Withdrawn

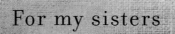

For my sisters

Little Red Riding Hood

Based on The Brothers Grimm tale

Illustrated by Debbie Lavreys

Clavis

NEW YORK

Once upon a time, there was a little girl who always wore a red cap, so everyone called her Little Red Riding Hood. She was loved by all because of her kindness and liveliness, but her grandmother, who lived in the woods, loved her most of all.

One day, Little Red Riding Hood's mother asked her to bring Grandma a basket with a bottle of cider and a piece of pie. Grandma was sick and a visit from her beloved granddaughter would certainly make her feel better. Little Red Riding Hood's mother warned her to stay on the road and not to wander into the woods. Little Red Riding Hood promised to be careful.

*L*ittle Red Riding Hood had just reached the woods when she met a wolf. She wasn't afraid of him, for she loved all animals and didn't know that wolves can be dangerous. The wolf greeted her and asked her where she was going.

"I'm bringing a bottle of cider and a piece of pie to my grandma. She's sick," Little Red Riding Hood replied.

"Where does your grandma live?" asked the wolf.

"Down the road, in a cottage behind a brick wall and an iron gate," Little Red Riding Hood answered, not knowing that the wolf was hatching a plan.

The wolf wanted to arrive at Grandma's before Little Red Riding Hood, so that he could eat the old woman for dinner, and have the young girl for dessert.

"Look at the beautiful flowers over there. Why don't you pick a bouquet for your grandma?" the wolf said.

Little Red Riding Hood looked to where the wolf was pointing and saw all the beautiful flowers. Grandma will be so happy when I give her pretty flowers, thought Little Red Riding Hood, and she wandered off the road.

Little Red Riding Hood was surrounded by the most beautiful flowers she had ever seen, they were everywhere she looked. Every time that she picked one, she saw another a little further away that was even prettier. Little Red Riding Hood wandered further and further from the road and into the woods forgetting about the wolf who had rushed straight to Grandma's cottage.

The wolf knocked on the door.

"Who's there?" Grandma asked.

"Little Red Riding Hood. I brought you a bottle of cider and a piece of pie. Can I come in?" the wolf said in a high pitched voice.

"Oh, it's you, Little Red Riding Hood. Please come in," Grandma answered happily.

The wolf opened the door, went into the bedroom, and swallowed Grandma up in one gulp. Then he put on one of her nightgowns and nightcaps, and got into her bed.

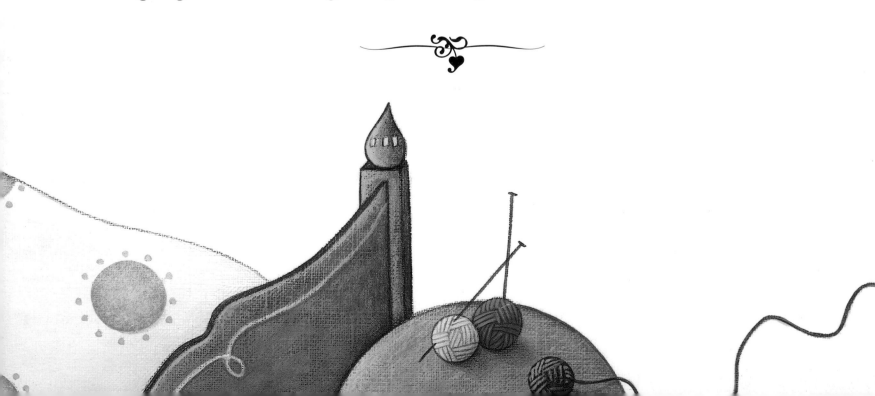

All this time, Little Red Riding Hood had been picking flowers and now her basket was full. She remembered her grandma and headed back to the road. When she reached the brick wall, she was surprised to see that the iron fence was open. And when she reached the cottage, she was surprised to see that the door was open as well. Little Red Riding Hood went inside and stood in front of the bed. Her grandma was lying there, but she looked so strange!

"Oh, Grandma, what large ears you have," said Little Red Riding Hood.

"The better to hear you with, my dear."

"Oh, Grandma, what large eyes you have."

"The better to see you with, my dear."

"Oh, Grandma, what large hands you have."

"The better to hold you with, my dear."

"Oh, Grandma, what a large mouth you have."

"The better to eat you with, my dear."

The wolf jumped up from the bed and swallowed Little Red Riding Hood up in one gulp. Then he lay down and went to sleep. He snored so loudly that a hunter passing by could hear it outside. Knowing that an old woman lived in the cottage, the hunter was concerned. He went inside and walked to the bed, where he saw the wolf.

The clever hunter suspected that the old woman might have been swallowed by the wolf and might still be alive in its belly. He took a pair of scissors and began to snip. A red riding hood appeared. And out jumped a girl. A nightcap appeared. And out jumped an old woman. How happy Grandma and Little Red Riding Hood were that the hunter had saved them!

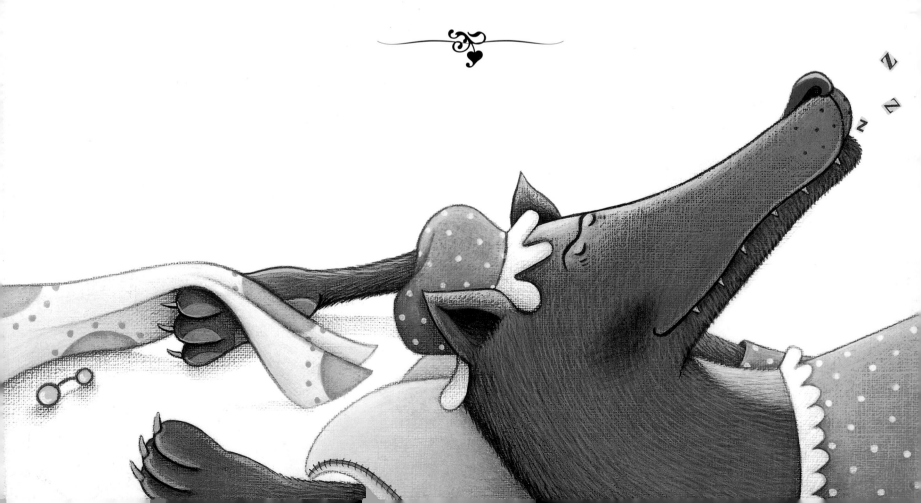

While the wolf was still asleep, the hunter placed several heavy stones in its belly. A little while later, when the wolf awoke and tried to run away, he could barely move, and he dropped to the ground. The hunter took the wolf away with him. Grandma and Little Red Riding Hood drank the cider and ate the piece of pie. Grandma was already feeling much better. Little Red Riding Hood thought about her mother's warning and promised herself that she would never wander off the road again.

Little Red Riding Hood
Based on The Brothers Grimm tale
Illustrated by Debbie Lavreys
Translated from Dutch. Original title: *Roodkapje*

ISBN: 978 1 60537 007 1

Manufactured in China
First Edition
10 9 8 7 6 5 4 3 2 1